Jet

By

Dave and Pat Sargent

Illustrated by
Jane Lenoir

Ozark Publishing, Inc.
P.O. Box 228
Prairie Grove, AR 72753

45564

Sargent, Dave, 1941-
    Jet / by Dave and Pat Sargent ; illustrated by Jane
Lenoir. — Prairie Grove, AR : Ozark Publishing, ©2001.
    ix, 36 p. : col. ill. ; 23 cm.   (Saddle-up series)

    "Good attitude"—Cover.
    SUMMARY: In 1860, an ill-tempered jet black horse,
selected by a Pony Express rider, finds himself in a very
dangerous situation and wonders if being hateful is really a
good idea. Includes factual information on black horses.
    ISBN: 1-56763-615-2   (hc)
          1-56763-616-0   (pbk)

    1. Pony express—Juvenile fiction. [1. Pony express—
Fiction. 2. Horses—Fiction. 3. West (U.S.)—History—1860-
1890—Fiction. 4. Temper—Fiction.]   I. Sargent, Pat, 1936-
II. Lenoir, Jane, 1950- ill.   III. Title. IV. Series.

    PZ10.3. S243Jet 2001
    [E]—dc21   2001-001203

Printed in the United States of America

iv

Inspired by

shiny black horses we sometimes see grazing in fields beside the road. They are so sleek and muscular, and their hair shines like black silk.

Dedicated to

all horse lovers everywhere. Do you have a horse? If you do, we know you love to ride it. Does it run like the wind? Tell us, have you ever been thrown?

Foreword

Jet Black was a cavalry horse with a bad attitude. He had a hateful disposition. When he wasn't in the mood to work, he bucked and reared. He pawed the air with his hooves. He sometimes bit the other horses and kicked them on their legs. They laughed at him, and of course, that made him even madder. Jet said, "You are a bunch of losers!"

Things began to change for Jet when a man in buckskins showed up one day. The man chose Jet Black to be a horse for the Pony Express. Jet begins to worry when the man starts talking about how they will have to survive blizzards, Indian uprisings, mountain lions, and panthers!

Contents

Jet

If you would like to have the authors of the Saddle Up Series visit your school, free of charge, call 1-800-321-5671 or 1-800-960-3876.

One

The Pony Express

The wake-up call from a cavalry bugle pierced the silence of the early morning. Horses snorted and pawed the ground as soldiers came out of their tents grumbling and yawning. Jet put his ears back and stomped his hoof on the ground.

"I don't want to work today," the jet black horse growled.

He was standing in a corner of the corral by himself. He glared as the other horses looked at him and snickered.

1

"If you wouldn't be so hateful, Jet, we wouldn't laugh at you," a sorrel said.

Jet Black bucked and reared. He squealed and pawed the air with his front hooves.

"You are a bunch of losers!" he exclaimed. "I really don't care if you like me or not." Suddenly he trotted over to the flea-bitten dun, gave him a mean look, and bit him on the shoulder.

"Stop it, Jet Black. That hurts. Why are you so hateful?"

"Because I want to be hateful," Jet snarled. "What are you going to do about it?"

"But I wasn't bothering you," the dun replied. "You just may need a friend one of these days, Jet. You better start being nice."

The black horse glared at him and said, "I don't need any friends." He turned and looked at the rest of the herd before adding, "And I like being hateful. Do any of you losers want to make something of it?"

The flea-bitten dun and the other horses looked at one another and shook their heads sadly.

Suddenly a man dressed in buckskins approached the corral with a cavalry soldier at his side.

"That's the horse I was telling you about," the uniformed man said as he pointed to Jet Black. "He's a real fine horse, but he has a hateful disposition! He just doesn't get along with the other horses."

"Hmmm," the frontiersman said thoughtfully. "I don't care how bad an attitude he has. I just need a fast horse."

"Well," the soldier drawled, "Jet's fast all right. I think he'll do a real good job for the Pony Express. He won't have time to complain or act hateful."

"You're right about that," the frontiersman said. "This is 1860, and times are changing. Folks living in the west need to receive news from the east, and the Pony Express will deliver the mail at a fast pace."

"Yes," the soldier replied, "but can you survive the Indian uprisings, mountain lions, panthers, and the blizzards?"

Jet jerked his ears forward and looked at the frontiersman. Yipes! he thought. This is not sounding like any fun.

"We may lose a few riders and horses," the man in buckskins said, "but the mail must go through. Get the black horse ready. I need to have him at the outpost by noon today."

"Wow," the sorrel and the other horses whispered as the men left the corral. "The Pony Express does not sound like a very safe job."

The flea-bitten dun walked over and nuzzled Jet's neck. He said, "I'm sorry you have to leave, Jet. I like you even though you are hateful."

"Thanks, Gizmo," the black horse murmured. "It does feel kind of good having at least one friend."

"Just imagine how it would feel to have a bunch of friends," the wise horse said.

Moments later, a soldier entered the corral with a rope. He tossed the loop over Jet's head and led him from the corral.

"Oh boy," Jet Black groaned. "Hateful may have put me in a very dangerous situation. And there's nothing I can do about it now."

Within thirty minutes, Jet was being led away from the fort by the man in buckskins. He glanced at the corral full of horses as he trotted through the gate. He noticed that they were not snickering at him now. He felt that they were real sorry to see him leave on such a dangerous assignment.

Hmmm, Jet Black thought. I just don't understand them. I bit that chestnut the other day. I kicked that bay on the leg. I ran that appaloosa away from his feed the other night. I have really been hateful to that palomino, and Gizmo has been the object of my mean streak for a long time now. Yet they seem sad that I'm leaving. I wonder how they would feel if I had been nice to them?

"Oh well," he muttered as he looked across the prairie toward the distant mountains. "I've never needed them before, and I don't need them now!"

Two

Painted Indian Ponies

The men at the outpost were waiting for Jet. The frontiersman handed the lead rope to a young man standing near the corral.

"He doesn't look fast to me," the young man grumbled.

The frontiersman chuckled and said, "Let me tell you, if this black puts all his hateful disposition into energy, he'll set a new record for mail delivery."

The man led Jet into the corral and removed the rope from his neck.

"Those wild Indians will take
the ornariness out of you, Jet Black.
You won't have time to be mean."

Jet glared at him, but the man
just laughed and left the corral.

Less that three hours later, Jet was saddled and tied to a post near the cabin. He felt the tension among the men growing with each passing minute. Suddenly a horse and rider thundered toward the outpost.

"He's coming!" the rider shouted. "Get that black ready to run."

Jet looked at the rider's horse and asked, "What's all the excitement about? I don't see anything."

"You will," the horse replied. "And you better be ready to run when they get here."

"You can't tell me what to do," Jet snarled. "I'll do what I want."

"Yeah," the horse chuckled as he walked away from Jet. "Of course you will. Good luck on your first Pony Express run through wild Indians and even wilder animals."

Hate is a strong word to use, but Jet acted as if he hated other horses and most men. He definitely had a bad attitude. When he wasn't biting someone, he was pushing or kicking them, daring them to fight him. He was a bully all right. And no one knew why. Who knows? Maybe he was mistreated as a colt.

The sound of pounding hooves turned Jet's attention to the east. A horse was running top speed toward the outpost. His rider was waving a large leather pouch high in the air.

Two men grabbed the reins on Jet, holding him at a standstill as the gasping horse stopped beside him. The rider handed the leather pouch to a man and jumped to the ground. Jet's reins were passed to the rider, who leaped onto Jet's back.

"They told me this mail is extra important," the rider gasped. "We have got to get it to Fort Churchill, Nevada, right away."

The pouch was again put in the hands of the rider, and he kicked Jet into action. Extra important mail? Good grief! Jet thought as his ears went back and he leaped forward. Within seconds, the horse and rider were racing through the sagebrush toward the distant hills.

Jet Black was used to taking off slow and then gradually speeding up. But not this time. Nope, not today. The muscles in his neck and legs strained to lengthen each stride. His shiny black coat glistened beneath the afternoon sun, and his long mane and tail flowed gracefully back with the force of the wind.

Jet ran at top speed until his breathing became labored. Then the rider reined him into a fast trot.

"Yeah," Jet mumbled. "This is more like it. I was beginning to think this fellow was trying to kill me. I wasn't even energetic enough to work for the cavalry today. I just didn't realize how easy I had it with them."

About an hour later, the horse and rider approached a tall mesa. As Jet trotted over the sandy terrain below it, figures suddenly appeared on the horizon. Jet Black noticed that the horses did not have saddles. And all of them were decorated with red, white, and black paint. Then he saw that the riders had feathers in their hair, and their faces were also painted.

"You are on our land!" one of the horses screamed. "And we do not allow trespassers."

Before Jet Black had a chance to respond, his rider kicked him into action.

"Jet," he yelled. "Those are Indians! If you want to live, you better run farther and faster than you ever thought possible!"

As the painted Indian ponies raced down the hill toward him, Jet felt his heart pounding with fear. He knew without having to be told that a hateful disposition would not help this situation. And he also knew that the Indians meant business, and the mail would not be delivered if they had their way. The extra important mail must be delivered, and I would like this man on my back to arrive

safely into Fort Churchill, he thought
as he raced past the mesa.

The black horse felt a surge of power race through him, and his hooves moved even faster across the untamed countryside. For three long miles, the horse and rider did not look back. Jet noticed the warhoops and threatening voices of the horses were getting more distant, but he did not slacken his pace.

"Just a little way further, Jet," his rider yelled to him. "There's another outpost not far from here, and I'll trade you for a fresh horse."

"You got it," Jet gasped quietly. "I'm looking forward to that."

As the black horse raced around a bend, his eyes saw something in the distance. That must be the outpost. I can't quite make it out, but that must be it, he thought. I'm so happy to see it because I'm tired.

Moments later, Jet heard the rider groan.

"The Indians have been here. The outpost has been destroyed."

Three

The Burned-out Outpost

The sun was setting on the western horizon as Jet Black walked toward the smoldering buildings of the outpost. His rider dismounted and looked around for signs of life, but there were none. Finally he very gently patted Jet on the shoulder and said, "We have to keep going, Jet. Our lives and the delivery of the extra important mail depends on it. Get a drink from the horse tank and rest a minute. Then we'll go again."

Jet slowly nodded his head.

Then he went to the tank and drank the cool liquid. After quenching his thirst, he shook his body until the saddle squeaked and rattled.

"Okay, Boss," he muttered. "I'm not very rested, but I'm ready."

As Jet carried his rider through the blackness of night, coyotes howled their sad and lonely song. The moon slowly rose above the treetops, casting light upon the trail. Jet quickened his pace to a gallop, and as the moon rose higher, he once again hit a dead run. As mile after mile passed beneath him, he never once stopped. He walked, trotted, and ran in successive intervals, but he never stopped.

The moon slowly moved across the sky until it was resting on the western horizon. As the sun peeked through the mist of early morning, the rider reined him to a halt.

"We'll stop for a minute, Jet," he said. "I'm about to fall out of the saddle, and you must be exhausted."

The man sat down beneath a tree. Within seconds, he was asleep. Jet lowered his head and dozed.

Suddenly Jet heard a strange sound and opened his eyes. A pack of wolves was slowly circling the rider. Jet reared up on his hind legs and screamed a warning.

Jet's hooves lashed out at the snarling, snapping wolves. His teeth were barred as he struck at them time after time. The rider scooted closer to the tree as Jet pounded at the wild animals. His hooves found their target several times before the vicious animals backed away.

For nearly an hour, Jet watched for dangerous predators as the rider slept. Then once again Jet gently nudged him on the shoulder.

"Come on, Boss," he said quietly. "Let's get that extra important mail delivered. And then I can get some sleep."

The rider opened his eyes and smiled at Jet.

"Thanks a lot, black horse," he mumbled as he stood to his feet. "You are right to wake me. We have to get to Fort Churchill right away."

Before mounting, the man gave Jet a couple of pats on the shoulder and said, "You don't have a hateful disposition, Jet. I think you have a good attitude."

Jet smiled as the rider settled into the saddle on his back.

"I don't have a hateful attitude anymore," he mumbled. "I have found out that hateful is an unhappy way to live for everybody."

Hours later, Jet proudly trotted through the gates of Fort Churchill. Civilians and soldiers alike gathered around the horse and rider, laughing and congratulating them on a job well done. Moments later, the leather pouch was opened. A tall man cleared his throat, then read, "Abraham Lincoln has been elected president of the United States of America!"

Hmmm, Jet Black pondered as the saddle was carefully pulled off his back. I wonder where history would be without a hateful reformed black horse to deliver important news. Life is good!

Four

Jet Black Horse Facts

Black horses are very rare in most breeds. Black horses have black points and black bodies with no obvious hairs of other colors, although sometimes they will have white markings on the face and legs.

If you find a few light hairs on a black horse, it's still called a black. The body can even be a little lighter than the points. And some will have a rusty color when they spend a lot of time in the sun. But they turn black again when they shed.

A *jet black horse* has a body color that is the same pure black as the point color, even when it spends a lot of time in the sun.